Dear Parent:

Congratulations! Your child is taking the first steps on an exciting journey. The destination? Independent reading!

STEP INTO READING® will help your child get there. The program offers books at five levels that accompany children from their first attempts at reading to reading success. Each step includes fun stories, fiction and nonfiction, and colorful art. There are also Step into Reading Sticker Books, Step into Reading Math Readers, and Step into Reading Phonics Readers—a complete literacy program with something to interest every child.

Learning to Read, Step by Step!

Ready to Read Preschool–Kindergarten
• big type and easy words • rhyme and rhythm • picture clues
For children who know the alphabet and are eager to begin reading.

Reading with Help Preschool–Grade 1
• basic vocabulary • short sentences • simple stories
For children who recognize familiar words and sound out new words with help.

Reading on Your Own Grades 1–3
• engaging characters • easy-to-follow plots • popular topics
For children who are ready to read on their own.

Reading Paragraphs Grades 2–3
• challenging vocabulary • short paragraphs • exciting stories
For newly independent readers who read simple sentences with confidence.

Ready for Chapters Grades 2–4
• chapters • longer paragraphs • full-color art
For children who want to take the plunge into chapter books but still like colorful pictures.

STEP INTO READING® is designed to give every child a successful reading experience. The grade levels are only guides. Children can progress through the steps at their own speed, developing confidence in their reading, no matter what their grade.

Remember, a lifetime love of reading starts with a single step!

Published in the United States by Random House Children's Books, a division of Random House, Inc., New York, and simultaneously in Canada by Random House of Canada Limited, Toronto.

www.stepintoreading.com

Educators and librarians, for a variety of teaching tools, visit us at
www.randomhouse.com/teachers

Library of Congress Cataloging-in-Publication Data
Sadler, Marilyn.
P. J. Funnybunny camps out / by Marilyn Sadler ; illustrated by Roger Bollen. p. cm.
SUMMARY: Although P. J. and his friends refuse to let Donna and Honey Bunny go camping with them because "camping is not for girls," the girls follow and get proof that camping is hard work even for boys.
ISBN 0-679-83269-6 (trade) — ISBN 0-679-93269-0 (lib. bdg.)
[1. Camping—Fiction. 2. Sex role—Fiction. 3. Animals—Fiction.]
I. Bollen, Roger, ill. II. Title. PZ7.S1239 Pab 2003 [E]—dc21 2002013648

Printed in the United States of America 37 36

P.J. Funnybunny Camps Out

By Marilyn Sadler
Illustrated by Roger Bollen

Random House New York

P. J. Funnybunny had
three best friends.
One day, P. J. said,
"Let's go camping."

P. J. packed a tent.

Ritchie packed
four sleeping bags.

Buzz packed a flashlight.

And Potts packed the food.

"Can Donna Duck
and I come, too?"
asked P. J.'s little sister,
Honey Bunny.

"No," said P. J.
"Camping is not for girls."

Then P. J. and his friends set out. They hiked through the deep woods.

They hiked across a wide river.

They even climbed
a high mountain.

Ritchie was tired.
He let go of his wagon.

Bump. Bump. Bump. Bump.
Four sleeping bags bounced
down the mountain.

Splash. Splash. Splash.

Three sleeping bags floated down the river.

"Camping is hard work," they all said.
"Camping is not for girls."

"Let's camp here," said P. J.
They all pitched the tent.

"I'm hungry," said Buzz.

"I'm hungry," said Ritchie.

"I'm hungry, too," said P. J.

Potts was not hungry.
He had eaten all the food.

Soon it got dark.
P. J. told a ghost story.
It was such a
good ghost story that
P. J. even scared himself!
"It's a good thing
the girls aren't here,"
he said.

Then they heard a noise.
"Boooooooooooo..."
It sounded like a ghost!

P. J. and his friends
looked out of the tent.
Buzz shined his flashlight
over by the rocks.

He shined it
over by the trees.

He shined it over by
two ghosts standing...

GHOSTS!

P. J. and his friends
jumped up so fast,
they knocked down their tent.
The flashlight rolled away.

P. J. and his friends ran
down the high mountain.

They splashed
across the wide river.

They ran through
the deep woods.

They ran all the way
to P. J.'s house.

"P. J. Funnybunny!"
said his mother.
"What happened?"

"Our tent fell down!"
said P. J.
"Our sleeping bags
floated down the river!"
said Ritchie.

"My flashlight got lost!"
said Buzz.
"We ran out of food,"
said Potts.

But Honey Bunny and Donna knew the truth.

Do you?